# the
# Lady
# and the
# Cowboy

CHRISTINE ANNE WENGER

SIGNAL HILL™

PUBLICATIONS

This book is fiction. The author invented the names, people, places, and events. If any of them are like real places, events, or people (living or dead), it is by chance.

## Dedication

To the memory of my father, who read every evening as long as I can remember. To Mom, for always being there. And to Jim, the cowboy in my life.

**SIGNAL HILL™**

**PUBLICATIONS**

Copyright © 1997
Signal Hill Publications
An imprint of New Readers Press
U.S. publishing division of Laubach Literacy International
Box 131, Syracuse, NY 13210-0131

Printed in the United States of America

Illustration by Patricia A. Rapple
Original cover art by Gary Gray

9 8 7 6 5 4 3 2 1

Library of Congress Cataloging-in-Publication Data

Wenger, Christine Anne

The lady and the cowboy / Christine Anne Wenger.

p.  cm. — (Janet Dailey's love scenes)

ISBN 1-56853-029-3 (pbk.)
1. Readers for new literates. I. Title. II. Series: Dailey, Janet.  Janet Dailey's love scenes.

PS3573.E528L33    1997
813'.54—dc20                                    96-36727
                                                CIP

# Chapter 1

NEW YORK CITY
MAY 1880

"A letter for you from Wyoming, Miss Trask." The gray-haired postman handed her a white envelope. Caroline's heart lifted when she saw her father's big, bold handwriting.

She took a deep breath and opened the envelope carefully. The letters from her father brightened her lonely days. He would tell of the latest calf or foal being born. He would tell funny stories about the cowboys who worked on the ranch. Maybe, just maybe, this letter would say that she could come home. How she wished . . .

In every letter she wrote to her father, Caroline begged him to let her come home to Wyoming Territory. To their ranch, the Lazy Circle T. Right after her mother died, her father had sold some cattle. He used the money to send Caroline to boarding school in New York City.

Her parents had come to Wyoming from New York years before. When she turned 17, the headmistress found Caroline employment at the home of Lewis and Mary Foxworth. She was the governess to the two Foxworth children.

It had been seven years now that she had been away from the Lazy Circle T.

Seven long years. Though she begged her father to let her come home, he always gave the same reason why she couldn't. He was afraid the hard life would kill her as it did her mother. He always said that in his letters.

With a sad smile, Caroline carefully unfolded the new letter and read:

My dearest daughter Caroline,

Your last letter was a comfort to me. But I can't change my mind. I know you want to come home, but New York City has so much to offer you. Wyoming is a harsh land. Your mother died because of this land, and I don't want that to happen to you.

I lost a lot of cattle this past winter, and the ranch needs a lot of work. This year will not be an easy one. It's not a fit place for a lady like you are now. It wasn't fit for your mother. It's a place for cowboys, not ladies.

There is some good news. During spring roundup, there were more calves than usual. I'm hoping that when the little critters grow up they'll bring a good price.

My beautiful daughter, in this envelope is some money for you. It's never as much as I would like to send, but buy yourself a pretty dress or whatever else you need.

I almost forgot. Your horse, Rosebud, had a fine colt last week. We are calling him Buddy.

Old Doctor Bittle stopped by when I was writing this letter and he sends you his best. He said he'd mail this letter for me when he goes to town.

All my love, Your father,

*Carl Trask*

Tears streamed down Caroline's face as she read the letter again and again. Something was wrong.

Caroline was 11 years old when he sent her away, but she could ride and rope as well as the best cowboys. Her father had taught her how to shoot a gun, too. He joked that soon she'd be able to shoot the eye out of a rattlesnake 20 feet away. They'd been so happy together.

Then her mother died and she was sent away.

Caroline looked down at her light blue satin dress with the ruffled sleeves. She felt the dark blue satin bow at her neck that kept her hat in place. She didn't care about these fancy things. She longed to be back in Wyoming, wearing her brown split skirt and riding her horse, Rosebud. She longed to see the new colt Buddy, too.

She wondered how many cattle had died during the winter. It had to be a lot because her father sounded worried. The money he sent was less than usual.

Caroline read again the part about the doctor stopping by. She knew without a doubt that her father must be sick. Her father would never let a doctor get within a foot of him. He was sick, or Doc Bittle would never have been at the ranch.

She had to know what was wrong, and she couldn't wait for another letter.

"I must leave right away," she said, putting the letter back into the envelope. "Right now. I have to go to him."

Caroline stood and hurried toward the Foxworth home to pack and to announce her departure. It was a huge house—the Foxworths were very rich. She was well taken care of—in fact, she lived like a lady, as her father said.

But all she wanted—all she'd ever wanted—was to go home and be with her father on the ranch.

She had saved some money over the years, money that her father had sent her. She hardly spent any of it. She saved most of her governess stipend, too. With the money her father had just sent, she had enough at last.

Caroline packed some traveling dresses and a few items she would want in Wyoming. Then she slipped her father's last letter under the blue ribbon that held together all the letters he sent over the years. She carefully put the bundle into her carpetbag.

She took a last look around at her room. It was beautiful, but she never felt at home in it as she did at the Lazy Circle T with its colorful Indian blankets and its walls made out of logs.

Caroline took a last look out of the window. She had made many wishes on many stars from that window. All the wishes were to return home.

New York City couldn't compare to the rugged mountains, the open spaces, the deep blue sky, and the sight of cattle grazing on long grass.

Wyoming.

She was going home at last!

# Chapter 2

THE LAZY CIRCLE T RANCH
WYOMING TERRITORY

"We've been over this before, Raven. The ranch is yours, and that's my final word on it."

"Leave it to your daughter, Carl," the younger man answered.

"You know that I don't want her anywhere near this place," the dying man said. "Now get the heck out of here, and let a man die in peace."

Raven turned to leave. He hated to see his friend looking so old, so sick.

"Raven . . . wait. I had a will made out. The lawyer in town has it. I left it all to you. Promise me that you'll do as I ask?" Carl Trask looked up at him from his bed. Raven saw that his friend's eyes were red and that he was breathing hard. He wouldn't live much longer.

"Look, Carl, I've written those letters to Caroline for you for seven years now. I've read the letters she wrote back to you. You know she wants to come home. She asks you in every letter."

Raven sat down next to the bed.

"You know why I don't want her to live here," Carl said. "Look what it did to her mother."

Carl started coughing. Raven picked up a tin cup full of cool water. He held the cup up to Carl's mouth, and Carl took a deep sip.

"She's eighteen years old." Raven ran his fingers through his long, straight black hair. "She's a woman now, Carl. I can tell by her letters. She can make her own choice."

Raven was thinking how much he liked Caroline from her letters. He understood her. He, too, was very lonely. He knew he wanted her to come home.

Raven waited until Carl stopped coughing. "Get some rest, you old snake. I'll be back in the morning."

Raven got up and pulled another blanket over his friend. No, not just his friend. The man was more like a father to him. He turned to leave. "I'll be back in the morning, Carl. Sleep now."

"Raven?"

"Yes?"

"Just see that Caroline never wants for anything. Promise me?"

Raven didn't answer. "Answer me, Raven. I ain't dead yet."

"You should leave it to Caroline. You know how much she loves this ranch. It's her home. But I don't want to fight with you about it. I promise."

"Promise me something else." Carl spoke so quietly, it was hard to hear him.

"Just name it," Raven said.

"Tell Caroline I love her. Tell her for me in the next letter."

"I tell her in every letter. Get some rest now, partner."

Raven heard Carl's heavy breathing and knew he was asleep.

"All Caroline wanted was to be with you, Carl. That's all. Looks like she's not going to get that wish," he whispered. "Good-bye, my friend."

Raven shut off the lantern and left the cabin. He decided not to ride back to his own ranch, Raven's Nest, tonight.

He had inherited the ranch after his father died.

Raven was surprised that he got the ranch. He and his father, Charles, had fought when Raven was a teenager. Charles had forced Raven to leave.

Raven always thought that his father felt guilty about the fight. Perhaps the ranch was his way of making up for all those lonely years.

Raven sighed. Soon he was going to own two ranches: one left to him out of guilt and one out of love. He, John Raven, was going to be the owner of one of the biggest spreads in Wyoming Territory.

He knew he should be happy, but he wasn't. Caroline Trask called the Lazy Circle T home. It was hers by rights.

He took a deep breath to clear his head. Spreading out his bedroll, he lay down and looked up at the stars. He wanted to be nearby in case Carl needed him.

# Chapter 3

DRY CREEK
WYOMING TERRITORY

The train pulled into Dry Creek's small railway station. Caroline was glad that the long train ride to Wyoming was over at last. She stood up and stretched her tired muscles as the train stopped. She stepped down onto the crowded platform of the train station.

Slowly Caroline looked around, drinking in the landscape she had dreamed of. She smiled at the snow on the mountains in the distance and took a deep breath of the fresh, clean air. The sun was shining and the sky was a beautiful blue, just as she knew it would be.

A tall, dusty cowboy in a big hat spit on the dirt near Caroline. "Why, howdy, young lady," he said to her. "What's a pretty lady like you doing alone in Dry Creek?" He leered at her.

Caroline didn't answer and stepped back from him. She wasn't used to these rough ways any longer.

She felt afraid, and looked around in panic. Suddenly another man was standing beside her.

Caroline looked at the tall man who had appeared. He wore a black linen duster, a black shirt unbuttoned at the neck, and black pants. Brown boots came almost up to his knees.

Hair as black as night blew around his shoulders in the breeze. His eyes were as blue as the spring sky above.

*He is handsome, so very handsome,* Caroline thought. *And somehow wild looking.* Yet she felt safe again. She hoped he was the sheriff.

"Zeke, what's going on here?" The man's blue eyes sparked with anger. "It looks like the lady wants to be left alone," he said. His voice was low and deep, and he spoke in such a way that no one would dare cross him.

Caroline smoothed down the sleeves of her dress. She looked up, and her eyes met those of the handsome stranger. She felt her heart skip a beat. He touched the brim of his black hat, and nodded at her. "I'm sorry about that, Miss . . . ?"

"Trask. Caroline Trask. Are you the sheriff?"

His tanned face paled. "What did you say your name was?" he asked.

"Caroline Trask." Caroline wondered what she had said to upset him. "Are you the sheriff?" she asked again.

"No, I'm not, Miss Trask. I'm just a simple cattle rancher." He let out a long, low whistle and shook his head.

She wondered why he was acting so strangely. "My father is Carl Trask. He owns the Lazy Circle T ranch. I haven't seen him in a long time, and I'm eager to get home."

He stared at her. "My name is John Raven, but most everyone just calls me Raven."

*Raven. The name fits him,* Caroline thought. *His hair is as black as a raven.* "If you'll excuse me, Mr. Raven, I must get to my father's ranch before sunset."

"It's just plain Raven, Miss Trask. There's no *Mister* in front of it."

Caroline smiled. "Thank you for coming to my assistance, Raven."

He tipped his hat. "He's not a bad man, Miss Trask. Just a little . . . rough.

Men around here are just not used to seeing a pretty lady like yourself."

She felt the warmth rush to her cheeks. "Thank you."

"How are you planning to get home, Miss Trask?" he asked.

"I was planning to rent a wagon from the livery."

"Why not use mine? It's right here in town," Raven offered. "I'll help you get to the Lazy Circle T safely," he added.

"You know where the Lazy Circle T is?" Caroline asked.

"Yes. Everyone in these parts knows the Lazy Circle T."

"Do you know my father?" Caroline asked.

"Yes. Very well," Raven said, then turned quickly and walked away before she could ask any more questions. And before she could refuse his help.

A short time later, he returned with a buckboard pulled by two chestnut horses.

Caroline insisted she could find her way home without his help. In her mind, she had pictured it a million times. The flat, green land. The mountains in the distance, the pine trees. This part of Wyoming was rugged, rough land. The people who worked the land and ran cattle had to be just as rough and rugged.

Like Raven.

She looked up at him. His smile was friendly, but his eyes held some sorrow.

Raven put his hands on her waist and helped her into the wagon. His hands were big and strong, and the feel of them made her heart beat wildly. She brushed back the curls that had escaped her hat and smoothed down her dress, trying to steady her breathing.

When he handed her the reins their fingers touched. What was it about this man that warmed her blood so and made her heart pound hard in her chest?

Caroline stammered a "thank you" before she lightly snapped the reins on the horses' rumps. The wagon creaked as it moved forward.

She smiled. This wasn't so hard.

Caroline looked back. Raven was watching her.

She forced her eyes back on the dirt road and pushed the handsome man out of her mind. Her thoughts turned back to her father instead. How she longed to know he was well. She couldn't wait to see the look on his face when he saw her after all these years.

Her thoughts were broken by the sound of a horse galloping. Fear hit her until she saw who it was. Raven. He slowed his big black horse to a trot alongside the wagon.

He touched the brim of his hat again.

"Miss Trask, you'd get there faster if you went in the right direction. The Lazy Circle T ranch is south, and you're heading east! Let me ride with you."

# Chapter 4

Raven didn't know how to tell Caroline her father was dead. He could see how happy she was to be going home at last. He didn't want to make her sad so soon.

He could tell by the way Caroline raised her face to the spring sun that she loved this land. She had pulled her hat off, and most of her golden hair had escaped from her bun and was blowing in the breeze. The dust from the road didn't seem to bother her one bit. Her green eyes twinkled with joy.

"Isn't it just beautiful here, Raven? Only horses and cattle as far as the eye can see. No high buildings to block your view. Just this land rich with wildflowers that spring up out of nowhere, and mountains so close you feel you can touch them," Caroline said.

*If Carl had just let her come home for a visit, he would have seen how much she loved this land,* Raven thought.

"Father always said that this land killed my mother, and I tried to convince him that he was wrong. She loved it here as much as I did. He said he should never have taken her away from New York City and brought her to Wyoming after they were married. Then there would have been a doctor close by when she needed one."

Caroline wiped a tear from her eye. "She died giving birth," she said. "Both my mother and the baby died."

"I know," Raven sighed. "Carl told me."

Raven just couldn't find the words to tell Caroline that her father was dead now, too. Nor that he was the new owner of the Lazy Circle T.

Finally, when the log cabin was in sight, he knew he couldn't wait any longer.

"Um . . . Miss Trask . . . Caroline . . . I have to tell you something," he said.

But Caroline didn't hear him. She had already jumped down from the wagon and started running toward the house. "Father!" she called out. "Father! It's me! It's Caroline! I'm home!"

Raven jumped off his horse and hurried toward Caroline. "Wait! Caroline, wait!"

Caroline looked up at the top of the hill beside the house and stood still.

Raven saw her shoulders shake with sobs the second she saw the fresh grave next to her mother's grave. She knew.

"I'm sorry, Caroline. I tried to tell you," he said. "I tried, but I just couldn't." She stared at him and said nothing. She looked back at the grave.

Raven walked toward her. "I buried Carl next to your mother. He died just one week ago today. I sent you a telegram, but I guess you had already left New York."

She knelt down when she reached the graves. Raven took his hat off and stood behind her.

The dirt on Carl's grave was fresh. Nothing grew on it but a couple of small weeds. Caroline reached for a weed and crushed it in her hand.

After several minutes, she said, "Raven, did you make the cross and carve his name on it?"

"Yes. I did."

"Thank you." She sniffed and pulled a handkerchief from the sleeve of her dress. "You did a beautiful job."

"Carl was like a father to me." Raven cleared his throat and helped Caroline up. "I've missed him."

Caroline wiped her eyes. "I've missed him for seven years, but I knew him through the letters he wrote. His letters kept him close to me."

"He couldn't wait to get a letter from you." Raven put his hat back on.

"Really?" Caroline asked.

"He would read them to me over and over," he lied.

"He did?"

"Yes. And his last words were of you. He said, 'Tell Caroline I love her.'" At least that part was the truth.

Fresh tears started flowing down her face. "Oh, no. Oh, God . . . why?"

She slumped forward. Raven caught her and held her in his arms. He held her gently as she cried.

She felt good in his arms. He had dreamed of holding her just like this. But in his dreams, she wasn't sad.

Caroline moved away from him, looking uncomfortable. He wanted to reach for her again, but it wasn't the right time.

"How did you know my father?" she asked.

"We're neighbors. My ranch, Raven's Nest, is the next one over. Carl took me in and gave me a job when my own father slammed the door in my face," Raven said.

"Your father sent you away, too?" Caroline asked.

"We had a terrible fight when I was young." His eyes looked sad as he remembered. "I worked for Carl for a few years," he went on. "Then my father sent for me. He had heard I was here. By then, he was sick, so I took care of running things for him. By the time my father died, we had made peace with each other. He left me the ranch."

He looked into her dark green eyes. She suddenly looked pale. Her face turned as white as the snow on top of Hawk Mountain. Something was wrong with Caroline. He stepped closer to her.

"Everything has been just so . . . so . . . overwhelming," she said. "The trip, my father's death . . ."

Raven caught Caroline easily as she fainted. He carried her toward the cabin. She was as light as a feather.

He couldn't stop looking at her. She seemed almost peaceful. He felt uneasy. He knew her peace wouldn't last long when she found out that Carl didn't leave her the Lazy Circle T.

Raven gave the old wood door a push with his boot and entered.

He put Caroline down on Carl's bed. He thought that he should loosen her dress and take off her shoes. It would help get her blood flowing again.

The shoes were no problem. He got them off as quickly as he roped and branded a calf. His big fingers took a while to undo the little pearl buttons on the front of her dress. Caroline's breath felt warm against his fingers.

Slowly, her eyes opened. The events of the day all came rushing back to her. Fresh tears sprang to her eyes, and she tried to wipe them away before Raven noticed.

Caroline was shocked to see that her buttons were undone. She reached for a patchwork quilt on the edge of the bed, but Raven got it first and spread it over her. "I remember my mother making that," she said simply.

In seconds, she was fast asleep.

Before he left the cabin, Raven couldn't stop himself from kissing her on the forehead. He felt as if he had known her forever.

In a way, he had.

# Chapter 5

The hot sun on her face woke Caroline up. It shone through the dusty windows of the cabin. For a moment, she didn't know where she was, then she remembered clearly. She was in Wyoming, her father was dead, and she had a ranch to take care of.

She rubbed her eyes, took a deep breath, and looked around the cabin. Not much had changed in the years that she had been gone. The yellow curtains with tiny blue flowers that her mother had made still hung on the windows. The rocking chair was in its usual spot by the fireplace.

Caroline noticed her father's things. His hunting rifle leaned against its usual corner of the cabin. His shooting irons, a pair of Colts, were still in his worn leather gunbelt hanging from a peg on the wall by the door. His coat hung from another peg.

Tears flooded her eyes as she remembered how happy they had been. Then her mother had died, and everything changed.

Caroline knew that her father sent her away out of love, but she still felt cheated of those seven years. Now he was gone too, and she was all alone.

She wiped her tears away. The small cabin wasn't the big Foxworth place, but it was home, and it was hers to care for. First, it needed a good scrubbing.

But before she tackled that, Caroline wanted to take a look around.

"I thought you were never going to wake up!" said a deep, male voice.

Caroline's heart skipped a beat. "What? Who?" she said, then she remembered. John Raven. Raven.

He peeked around the door, then walked right in, as bold as a hungry bear.

Raven handed her a tin cup. She reached for it as calm as could be, as if a man handed her a cup of coffee in bed every day.

"What are you doing here?" Caroline asked.

"I camped by the creek."

Caroline looked down, and saw that the front of her dress was open. Quickly, she pulled the patchwork quilt under her chin. She felt suddenly ashamed.

"Please step out while I dress," she asked shyly.

He tugged on his hat brim as he always did. "Yes, ma'am."

He smiled as he set his cup of coffee down on the table. Caroline could hear the noise of his boots as he walked across the front porch then down the steps. He was whistling.

Caroline jumped out of bed, dressed quickly, and combed her hair. She looked around for a bucket of water to wash her face, but there was none. She headed outside to the pump.

Caroline couldn't believe that she had slept so long. She remembered how Raven unbuttoned her dress, and her heart beat faster as she thought of his gentle touch, and the feel of his large fingers brushing against her. Her face became warm again, and her stomach fluttered like a hummingbird.

As she walked back toward the cabin from the pump, the object of her thoughts moved toward her.

"There are some things that need to be fixed around here," Raven said, pointing at the barn.

"I know. I was just going to see what needs tending to first," Caroline said. "My father must have been sick a long time to let things go the way they have. Was he, Raven?"

Raven didn't have the heart to tell her that the Lazy Circle T barely broke even from year to year. That the men who worked on the ranch had long ago been dismissed. She could never know that he was the one who sent her money when Carl didn't have it.

"Carl was sick on and off for a long time," Raven said.

"I wish I'd known. I would have come home much sooner. You were his friend, Raven. I wish you had told me."

"Carl didn't want that."

Raven realized that he was just as concerned about Caroline as Carl had been. "You shouldn't be out here alone.

When word gets out that you are by yourself, every no-good saddle tramp and outlaw will ride by. I don't like it."

"Thank you for worrying about me, but I know how to use a gun, and I can take care of myself."

"When did you learn how to use a gun?" he asked.

"My father taught me before he sent me away," Caroline explained.

"You were eleven years old! Have you shot since then?" Raven asked, his voice a little louder than necessary.

"No."

"Could you shoot a man if you had to? Or a wild animal?" He was shouting now. "I'm worried about you being out here all alone. There's a lot you don't know, Caroline."

"I'll learn," she said, putting her hands on her hips. "Raven, I thank you for your concern, but I'm not a weak woman. I may look like a lady after my years away. But this ranch is in my blood. I can work the land and take care of this place as well as any man. It's all I thought about during those lonely years away from home."

"You think you can run this ranch all alone?"

"I am sure going to try."

"I told you that you need help," Raven said. "I can't stay out here all the time. I have a ranch to run."

"I don't need any help, and no one asked you to stay here."

Raven crossed his arms and shook his head. "Just like you didn't need any help in town? What if that man showed up when you were alone?"

She turned away and didn't answer.

"Caroline, if it's money you need, I can help you. I promised your father I'd take care of you," Raven said.

Before he could say any more, Caroline changed the subject. "Raven, are those the Lazy Circle T cattle? I can't see the brand from here."

"They have my brand, Caroline. Those are my cattle grazing out there."

"Then where are the Lazy Circle T cattle? And where is my horse, Rosebud, and where is Buddy, Rosebud's new colt?"

"Um . . . uh . . . I'm taking care of your cattle and Rosebud and Buddy. I moved them to my ranch when Carl died," Raven mumbled.

"Well, thank you, but you can bring them back now. I can take care of them. If need be, I'll hire some help."

Raven shook his head. His long black hair moved about his shoulders. "No, Caroline. It's just too much for you now."

His blue eyes showed his concern along with something else, something that made Caroline's pulse race.

"I am grateful for all you've done, but please don't worry about me anymore," she said. "Now if you'll excuse me, I have things to do here. I'm sure that you have things that need tending at Raven's Nest. Won't your family be missing you by now?"

"No one will miss me," he said quietly.

His eyes gave him away. Caroline realized that Raven was lonely, too. She didn't know what to say, so she changed the subject again. "Well, if you'd be so kind as to bring back my cows, I'll bother you no more."

He raised an eyebrow. "What if I buy your cows from you, and you can go back to New York? Or you can stay in town. You could buy a nice house there with the money I'd give you for them."

Caroline was disappointed. She was sure Raven understood how much the ranch meant to her. "But this is my home. It means everything to me. I've been away for so long. I'm never leaving again."

"I will see that you get a good income no matter where you live. I promised Carl that I would take care of you, and I never break a promise."

"And that's how you would take care of me? By sending me away? That's just what my father did." Tears welled up in her eyes. "Well, I'm not going, mister. I'm staying here on my ranch. Now, when are you going to bring me my cattle and my horses?"

"I'll return with your cows at roundup time in the fall. They are mixed in with several other herds, so I can't return them to you now," Raven answered.

She had to admit that she was glad she didn't have to take care of them right now. Fixing up the cabin and the barn would require all her time.

"Fine," she said.

"I'll come by in a few days with Rosebud and Buddy and see how you're doing," Raven said.

"Thank you."

"Good-bye, Caroline." He tugged at the brim of his hat, easily mounted his horse, and trotted away from her.

"Good-bye. And thank you, Raven."

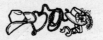

She watched him ride away until she couldn't see him anymore. She already felt lonely without him. Even the day seemed to lose its sunshine.

He was such a strong man, yet he was gentle with her. He was also the handsomest man she had ever laid eyes on. He made the gentlemen in New York City seem very dull.

He probably had all the women in Dry Creek chasing him.

Caroline walked toward the cabin to change out of her dress and put on her father's work clothes.

She had a lot of work to do today, and she was going to enjoy it.

# Chapter 6

Two hours after Raven left, Caroline
admitted that she did need help around
the ranch. A lot of help.

Two days later, when she looked at
the growing list of things to be done,
she knew she was in trouble.

She was too proud to say it out loud,
but deep in her heart, Caroline knew
that Raven was right. She couldn't do it

all. The heavy rain the night before proved that the cabin needed a new roof. So did the barn.

As much as she didn't want to, Caroline had to go back to Dry Creek and go to the bank. She needed a loan to buy some supplies. She would have to hire some men to fix both roofs and make some other repairs.

She would buy some corn seed. She wondered if it was too late in the season to plant. She didn't know, but she would certainly find someone to ask in town.

She was so tired of eating canned beans and peaches. Chickens. She needed some chickens for eggs. She closed her eyes and dreamed of fried chicken.

She understood she had forgotten a lot in seven years. Her parents had taken care of so many things for her. There was a lot she didn't know. That was hard to admit.

Caroline also would never admit to anyone that she was scared of being alone, especially at sunset.

The howling of the wolves and the other night sounds scared her. She hadn't had a good night's sleep since Raven left. She was alone as far as the eye could see. Raven was her nearest neighbor, and he was miles away.

Caroline missed her father. She also thought of Raven often. She missed him, too. She missed his smile and his laugh. She liked his low, deep voice and the way he sometimes teased her. She wanted to get to know him better.

She tried to put Raven out of her mind. There were too many other things to think about and do!

Right now, she needed a loan.

The drive to town was hot and dusty. All Caroline could think of was taking a nice cool dip in the creek. She loved to listen to the water rush over the stones. She was beginning to forget the luxuries of New York City life.

Caroline left the wagon at the Dry Creek Livery. She'd have to return the horses and wagon to Raven soon, but until then, she was glad to have them.

She walked to the bank and asked to speak to someone about a loan. Soon a short, skinny man with glasses and a head of pure white hair appeared.

"I am Sidney Greengate, the bank manager. What can I do for you, young lady?" he asked.

His smile was friendly and warm, and he smelled of peppermint and cigar smoke.

"I'm Caroline Trask. You may have known my father, Carl Trask."

"I sure did, Miss Trask. I was sorry to hear about his death. He was a good man—a very good man."

"Thank you, Mr. Greengate."

"Your father talked about you every time I saw him. I'm going to miss him. Yes, Carl Trask was a good man." He led her to a door with *Bank Manager* on it in black letters. "What can I do for you, Miss Trask?"

"I would like to take out a loan. It will only be for a little while, you understand. I will pay you back when my cattle go to market."

He didn't answer, but opened the door to his office.

"Sit down, please." He pointed to a large wooden chair, and Caroline sat down.

He took a seat behind his big wood desk and pulled a piece of paper from the top drawer. He dipped his pen in ink and waited. "I'd like to help you, Miss Trask. Now, how much would you like to borrow and what do you intend to use as collateral?"

"Collateral?" Caroline asked. "What's that?"

"Something of value you put up to insure you will pay the bank back," Mr. Greengate said. "If you don't pay the loan back, I take your collateral."

"My cattle. I will put my cows up as collateral."

The banker shook his head. "I have more cattle put up as collateral than all the stars in the sky, Miss Trask. I can't take any more."

"I'll put up the Lazy Circle T then." Caroline nodded. "I'll put up my ranch."

Mr. Greengate put his pen down and leaned back in his chair. "But it's not yours to put up," he said quietly.

Caroline's mouth dropped open. "What did you say?"

Mr. Greengate let out a deep breath. "I'm so sorry. I thought you knew."

"I don't understand, Mr. Greengate. What are you talking about?" Caroline found herself getting warm. Her heart beat fast. Something wasn't right.

"I thought you knew," Mr. Greengate said again.

Caroline's voice shook. "Who is the owner of the Lazy Circle T if I'm not?"

The banker answered reluctantly.

"John Raven owns the Lazy Circle T. Your father left it to him in his will."

"Raven! I don't believe it." Caroline shook her head and blinked back tears. "Why would my father leave the ranch to Raven and not to me?"

"You'll have to ask Mr. Raven that, Miss Trask." The banker stood up. "I wish there were something I could do."

"Just tell me who has my father's will, Mr. Greengate. I want to see it with my own eyes." Caroline stood up. She felt dazed and confused. She needed to get some air.

"Eli Hart, the lawyer. His office is across the street," said Mr. Greengate, opening the door for her.

# Chapter 7

Caroline knocked. She pushed opened the door to Eli Hart's office and found a man sitting behind a desk. He was bent over some papers and didn't notice her come in.

"Mr. Eli Hart?"

He looked up, surprised. He peered over his glasses at Caroline. "Yes. Who are you? What do you want?"

"I'm Caroline Trask. I'd like to see my father's will."

"Oh, Miss Trask . . . of course. I have the will right here." Mr. Hart reached into a drawer and handed Caroline some papers. "I was going to send these to you."

She read quickly. Her father had left everything to John Raven. Everything—the cattle, the house, the land. He also directed that John Raven was to see that she, Caroline Trask, was taken care of.

She looked at the big black X at the place where her father should have signed his will.

Caroline was puzzled. "Mr. Hart, my father didn't sign this. This isn't his signature."

"It certainly is, Miss Trask. I saw him make that X myself. As you can see, I signed as witness," the lawyer said.

Caroline looked at the X again. "But why didn't he sign his name?"

"Because Carl Trask couldn't read or write, that's why."

Caroline shook her head. "That can't be. My father wrote many letters to me. I have them at home. I can show you." Her voice shook with anger.

The lawyer stood. "I'm telling you that Carl Trask couldn't read or write. I wrote this will. He told it to me and I wrote it. He left everything to his neighbor, John Raven."

"I wish to see a judge, Mr. Hart," Caroline said.

"This isn't the big city, Miss Trask. The judge makes his rounds on horseback." Eli Hart checked some papers on his desk. "But you're in luck. Judge Parker will pass through here in about a month."

"Fine. I will see him then," Caroline said, wondering if she had enough money to last that long. "Thank you and good-bye, Mr. Hart."

She left his office and walked onto the dusty street. Caroline felt as if she had been run over by a herd of wild horses. Questions buzzed in her head.

*Who wrote all those letters if my father didn't? Why didn't he leave me the ranch? And why did Raven let me make a fool of myself and think the ranch was mine?*

As she rode home, more questions nagged at her mind.

*Where am I going to live now? And what about Rosebud and the colt, Buddy? Are they Raven's too?*

She let the tears fall down her face. No one was there to see her cry on the long, dusty trail back home.

Home? No. It wasn't her home anymore. It was Raven's home.

"How could you do this to me, Father?" Caroline sobbed.

No one answered. There was just the creak of the team pulling the wagon.

Raven's wagon. It all was Raven's.

What was she going to do?

# Chapter 8

When she came over the last hill, Caroline saw Raven on the roof of the cabin. He was hammering. He wasn't wearing a shirt, and with every swing of the hammer, muscles bulged in his back and arms. His hat was off, and his long, black hair was tied back with a thin strip of leather.

He saw her coming toward him. "Hello, Caroline. All that rain last night reminded me that your roof was probably leaking. I thought I'd fix it."

She shaded her eyes from the hot afternoon sun and said, "You mean *your* roof, don't you?"

He didn't answer for a while, then climbed down the ladder and walked toward her. "You know?" he asked softly.

"I went to town today. I saw Mr. Greengate, the banker, and Mr. Hart, the lawyer," Caroline said, looking into his sky-blue eyes. "They say that the Lazy Circle T is yours."

"But you don't think so, Caroline?"

"No, I don't. There is no way that my father would sign with an X when he wrote me so many letters. I have my father's letters, Raven. I am going to present this matter before the judge when he comes through here. I'll show him the letters, and let him decide who owns this ranch, me or you."

"Carl did leave me the ranch, Caroline. I tried to talk him out of it, but you know he didn't want you here in Wyoming. That's why he didn't leave it to you," Raven said.

Raven looked away, then sighed. "Caroline, I am just following Carl's wishes. This ranch doesn't mean anything to me, other than it was his and he was good to me."

"And it means everything to me." She turned to leave. "I'll see you in court, Mr. Raven. Now get off my land."

She didn't mean to yell, but everything was going wrong. This was not how she dreamed things would happen. Not at all.

He raised an eyebrow. "This ranch is mine, until the judge says otherwise, and I'm not about to let it fall apart. I am going to fix this roof, and you can either help or get out of my way."

"Are you going to throw me out of the cabin, too?" she asked, turning away. She hoped he wouldn't throw her out. She had nowhere else to go.

"Of course not." Raven gently took her elbow and turned her around. "Look, until this is settled, how about if we work together? Whether the judge says the ranch is mine or yours, I'd like it still to be standing." He smiled. "I'm sure you feel the same way."

"I do."

"May the best man, or woman, win," he said.

Caroline tried to tell herself that she shouldn't be mad at Raven. It wasn't his fault that her father's stubbornness caused all this.

"You're right. Let's work together until then. I'll go change into work clothes," Caroline said.

Perhaps working would take her mind off things.

# Chapter 9

Caroline came out of the house wearing Carl's trousers and one of his shirts. She and Raven continued working on the roof. Caroline learned fast and soon was swinging a hammer with skill.

A few days later, they started putting a new roof on the barn. A few days after that, they planted corn and hay. Caroline planted some vegetable seeds that she had found in the barn.

Some evenings, Raven rode to his ranch from the Lazy Circle T to check the cattle. Most nights, he camped by the creek. He drove the team to Dry Creek for supplies a few times each week. Every time he left, he couldn't wait to get back to Caroline.

They talked for many hours as they sat by the creek under the stars. But they never talked about who really owned the Lazy Circle T.

One Monday, the law clerk Josh Jenkins rode out and brought Caroline a letter from Eli Hart.

The letter stated that Judge Parker would hear Caroline's case on Tuesday at nine o'clock in Eli Hart's office. John Raven was to attend also.

That night Caroline and Raven ate in silence.

"Shall we ride in to Dry Creek together in the morning?" Caroline finally asked after dinner.

"I think that's a good idea," Raven agreed. "I'll be back at sunrise."

He took a lantern from the hook and walked down the steps of the cabin.

Caroline hurried onto the porch. "Wait. I'd like to say something."

"I'm listening."

"These past five weeks have been happy, and it's because of you. I want you to know that if I win the case tomorrow, you are welcome here any time," Caroline said. Secretly, she hoped it would be often.

"It's been the best time of my life," Raven said. *And no matter what happens tomorrow, the ranch is yours*, he thought. *You've proved that you belong here. You love this land, and I want you to be happy.*

Raven wanted to take her in his arms. But he knew he couldn't—not yet. He also knew that he needed her. She filled the space in his lonely heart. He tugged his hat brim. "Tomorrow."

# Chapter 10

"Miss Trask, just sign here and the Lazy Circle T is yours," said Judge Parker.

"I don't understand," Caroline said, confused. "I thought we were going to have a court hearing to decide if the ranch is mine or Raven's."

"That's no longer needed. Mr. Raven has signed the Lazy Circle T over to you," replied Judge Parker.

The lawyer, Eli Hart, dipped a pen in ink and handed it to her. He pointed to where she was to sign on the paper.

Caroline turned and looked at Raven. "Why?"

Raven shifted his tall body in the hard wooden chair. "I can't take it away from you, Caroline. If Carl had seen how much you love the ranch and the land, he would have never left it to me."

Caroline stared at the paper before her. All she had to do was sign her name and it would all be hers.

She held the paper before her. Something wasn't right.

Caroline looked at the paper, then to her stack of letters tied with the blue ribbon, then back to the paper again.

Her heart pounded in her chest and her face flushed. The writing was the same on the letters as it was on the paper that would give her the ranch.

"You wrote those letters to me, didn't you, Raven?" she asked quietly. "You were the one who wrote me all those years, not my father."

"Yes," Raven admitted. "But most of the time Carl told me what he wanted to say. I just filled in the rest."

"My father didn't read you my letters. You read them to him," Caroline said. "Isn't that true, Raven?"

He nodded slowly.

"I feel so stupid. Stupid and foolish." Caroline sighed and smoothed down her dark green dress.

The judge snapped his law book shut. "Let's get out of here, Hart, and let these young people talk. We've got time before the next case."

Caroline and Raven now found themselves alone in Eli Hart's office.

"Carl didn't want you to know he couldn't read or write. He didn't want you to think less of him," Raven said.

Caroline looked up at him. "I would never think less of my father because of that." She stood up and looked out of

Eli Hart's window. "All my stupid talk about getting the ranch running—you knew I couldn't do it alone."

"I admired you," he said.

Raven walked toward her and held out his arms. He reached for her hand and gently pulled her close to him, into his arms.

"I love you, Caroline." She lifted her chin to look up at him, and he kissed her. It started as a soft whisper of a kiss, but when she put her arms around him and held him close, it deepened.

He heard a soft sound from Caroline, and his kiss became harder, stronger, until he knew he had to stop.

"I love you, too, Raven. I feel as if I've known you my whole life. The moment I met you, I felt that I'd been with you forever."

"I feel the same way, Caroline." His feelings were so strong that he could barely get the words out.

"I was so lonely in New York . . . so lonely." Caroline said softly.

"I know, Caroline. I know you were." Raven held her head tight to his chest and smoothed her hair. "I was lonely here. I lived for your letters."

His hand was warm on her cheek. "The letters—your letters—kept me from going crazy," Caroline said.

"It was the same for me. I fell in love with you through your letters, you know," Raven said.

Raven smiled and kissed her forehead. "You don't know how much I wanted to go to New York and meet you."

Caroline's heart beat with joy. "I think I fell in love with you the minute I saw you in Dry Creek," she said.

He smiled. "It's hard to believe that a lady like you could ever love a cowboy like me."

"Just tell me why you made me worry and wonder if I'd have a place to live?" Caroline asked.

"I was hoping to win your love before you ever found out." Raven began. "Then who owned the ranch wouldn't have mattered at all. But that didn't happen. I knew you wouldn't accept the ranch if I tried to give it to you. You're so strong and proud. It's part of why I love you. So I decided to make sure the place was fit to live in. That way, I got to help you and be with you every day."

"You're a smart man, Mr. Raven."

He picked her up and swung her around as she laughed. "Marry me, Caroline."

Caroline smiled. "I'd be proud to be your wife."

He kissed her softly at first, then hard. It was a kiss full of love and laughter and a promise of a long, wonderful life together. The lady and the cowboy—a perfect match.

Caroline knew that with Raven she would never be lonely again.